Kikuchi's Sushi

About the Author
Myung Sook Jeong has worked as a reporter in Australia and has written poems, fairytales, and picture books while traveling worldwide. Her other books include *Seeing World History Through Painting, First Step Art, First Step World History (Volumes 1 and 2), Pompidou Center, Pride of the Country,* and *National Treasure Story.*

About the Illustrator
Sul Hee Kook studied western painting in college, and has shown work in exhibitions such as "The Paper That Had Eaten a Story"(2007) and "Grow In"(2011). Her works include *Oh, Back Off Now; The Dream That Fly in the Sky; Where Did It Come From?; Let's Share a Warm Feeling; Yellow Mailbox;* and others.

Tantan Publishing Knowledge Storybook *Kikuchi's Sushi*

www.TantanPublishing.com

Published in the U.S. in 2017 by TANTAN PUBLISHING, INC.
4005 w Olympic Blvd., Los Angeles, CA 90019-3258

©Copyright 2017 by Dong-hwi Kim
English Edition

ISBN: 978-1-939248-17-6

Printed in Korea

Kikuchi's Sushi

Written by Myung Sook Jeong   **Illustrated by Sul Hee Kook**

✿ **TanTan Publishing**

Ohayou!

I'm a fox living in Hokkaido, Japan. "Ohayou" means
"good morning" in Japanese.
Look at what I am holding on top of this leaf.
It's a rice ball.
Doesn't it look tasty?
This rice ball is made by Grandpa Kikuchi.
Kikuchi is the owner of a sushi restaurant,
and he makes really delicious sushi—it's as if he uses
magic spells.
Let me tell you a story of Kikuchi and me.

3

I love watching over the village from the top of the hill.
But there is a very unusual house in the village.
People are always lined up,
and everyone walks out the door smiles and says,
"Kikuchi's sushi is absolutely delicious!"
I was really curious what sushi tasted like.
So I decided to visit Kikuchi's house.

4

Japan's Most Famous Food: Sushi

A long time ago, areas like Southeast Asia and China preserved fish in vinegar so that the fish would stay safe to eat for a long time. This custom was passed on to Japan. In the old days, cleaned fish and rice were placed together on a board with salt spread on it. Then a heavy stone was put on top of the food, and when the fish was fermented, it was ready to eat. As time passed, the process changed, and today's sushi is formed by mixing rice with vinegar and setting the unfermented fresh ingredients on top.

Late at night when all the customers had left,
I went to Kikuchi's sushi restaurant.
As I quietly opened the door, a small bell rang.
Jingle, jingle.
An old man was startled to see me.
It was Kikuchi.
I took out all the acorns that I had gathered.
"Kikuchi, I'll give you all of these acorns if you will please give me some sushi."
Kikuchi shook his head with his arms folded.
"Fox, I do not take acorns."
"I want to find out what sushi tastes like." I said.
Kikuchi thought deeply about this and said,
"If you find me the most delicious spring water, I will give you some sushi."

Foxes in Japanese Culture

The ancient Japanese considered nature and animals to be gods. They believed the fox was the god of grain and treated it as a sacred animal. Foxes are generally cute and clever in ancient Japanese tales and often appear as animals that bring wealth.

The most delicious spring water? That was a very
easy task.
I led him to a spring hidden in the deep valley.
"This spring has the sweetest and most refreshing
water," I said.
Kikuchi filled a bucket with spring water.
"Sushi," he told me, "tastes best when made with
fine rice and delicious water. I will make sushi for
you using this spring water."
Kikuchi used the spring water to cook rice and made
some sushi.
I put a tuna belly sushi into my mouth.
"Oh! So this is what sushi tastes like!"
I was delighted by the taste of sushi melting in
my mouth.

The next evening, I visited the sushi restaurant again.
Kikuchi greeted me gladly.
"Fox, are you here today to eat sushi again?" he asked.
"If you find me fresh wasabi, I'll give you sushi."
I was surprised by what Kikuchi said.
Wasabi was spicy enough to bring tears to my eyes.
But if I could trade it for Kikuchi's sushi, nothing else mattered.
I went into the woods at once to find the aromatic wasabi.

Wasabi and Japanese Food

Japanese food usually tastes plain, but additions that have a strong fragrance or flavor like wasabi, citrus, or ginger are sometimes incorporated. Wasabi, which has a sharp taste, is especially used with sashimi, sushi, and noodles, which are classic Japanese dishes. Fresh wasabi prevents sushi from spoiling and enhances the taste of the fish.

I found wasabi near the creek.
"Here! This wasabi is the most aromatic and fresh.
But does wasabi have to be put in sushi?"
"Of course!" Kikuchi answered. "It must be used.
Real sushi needs the stinging taste of the wasabi."

Kikuchi washed the wasabi thoroughly and grated it.
Then he carefully placed a pinch of finely grated wasabi
between the fish and the rice of the sushi.
"Oh!" I cried. "The spiciness makes me tear up, but
it is delicious!"
The combination of fragrant wasabi, fresh flounder and
salmon, and the firm grains of rice that came together
to form Kikuchi's sushi was simply the best.
Plus, the green tea made my stomach feel warm.

Sushi and Tea

While eating sushi, the fishy taste and grease can be
avoided by frequently drinking green tea. Tea brewed
from dried leaves is the most common, but powdered
tea (made from steamed tea leaves that are dried and
crushed) is also enjoyed by many people.

One sunny day, I visited Kikuchi's sushi restaurant again.
I noticed flags shaped like carp fluttering above
Kikuchi's restaurant.
"Is the carp sushi on the menu today? What are those
carp-shaped flags?"
"Those are called koinobori, which is a carp-shaped flag
hung on Children's Day. I hung it with a prayer that my
only grandchild will grow up healthy," Kikuchi told me.
"Seeing those flags makes me want to eat a carp."
I licked my lips while gazing at the carp flags.
"It is hard to make sushi out of carp," Kikuchi said.
"Let's catch an eel instead, and make savory eel sushi."
I went to the riverbank, following Kikuchi's lead.
It was already dark when we arrived at the river.

Kodomo No Hi and Hina Matsuri

Kodomo No Hi is a festival held to pray for young boys
to grow up healthy and smart. It occurs annually on
May 5th. Due to the belief that the carp energetically
swims up the river and becomes a dragon, the carp-
shaped flag is hung. Every year on March 3rd is the
Hina Matsuri, which is the day to celebrate young girls.
Each house covers its stairs in red fabric and families
place pretty dolls, cookies, peach flowers, and other
things on the steps.

15

"The moonlight is very bright."
Kikuchi hung a stone from a hollow bamboo branch
and dunked it in the river.
"Now the eel will hide itself inside this bamboo."
After a while, Kikuchi lifted the bamboo trap up high
and an eel really was flopping inside of it!
Kikuchi cleaned the freshly caught eel.
Then he baked it and spread dark brown sauce
several times on the eel.
The cooking smell was enough to make my
mouth water.
"This is a sushi made out of eel," Kikuchi said as he
gave it to me.
The eel sushi was tastier because of the syrupy sauce.

"Kikuchi!" I exclaimed. "Sushi is so delicious.
It is an easy dish to prepare, with only a few steps."
Kikuchi laughed out loud.
"You think sushi is an easy food to prepare?"
"Yes! You shape the rice,
add a pinch of wasabi,
and place the fish on top of it. Isn't that it?"
"Haha, Fox! Let's try making sushi."
Kikuchi put the white apron on me.
"Kikuchi, you can look forward to this!" I bragged.
I was excited at the thought of making sushi.

"Oh, no!"
The clump of rice fell from my hand in a big mess.
"Fox, the shape is important when you make sushi,"
Kikuchi told me.
After what Kikuchi said, I squeezed the rice grains.
"But if you squeeze the sushi too hard, the rice
becomes firm and tasteless," he told me. "On top
of that, the fish becomes less fresh because the
temperature of your hand makes the fish warm."

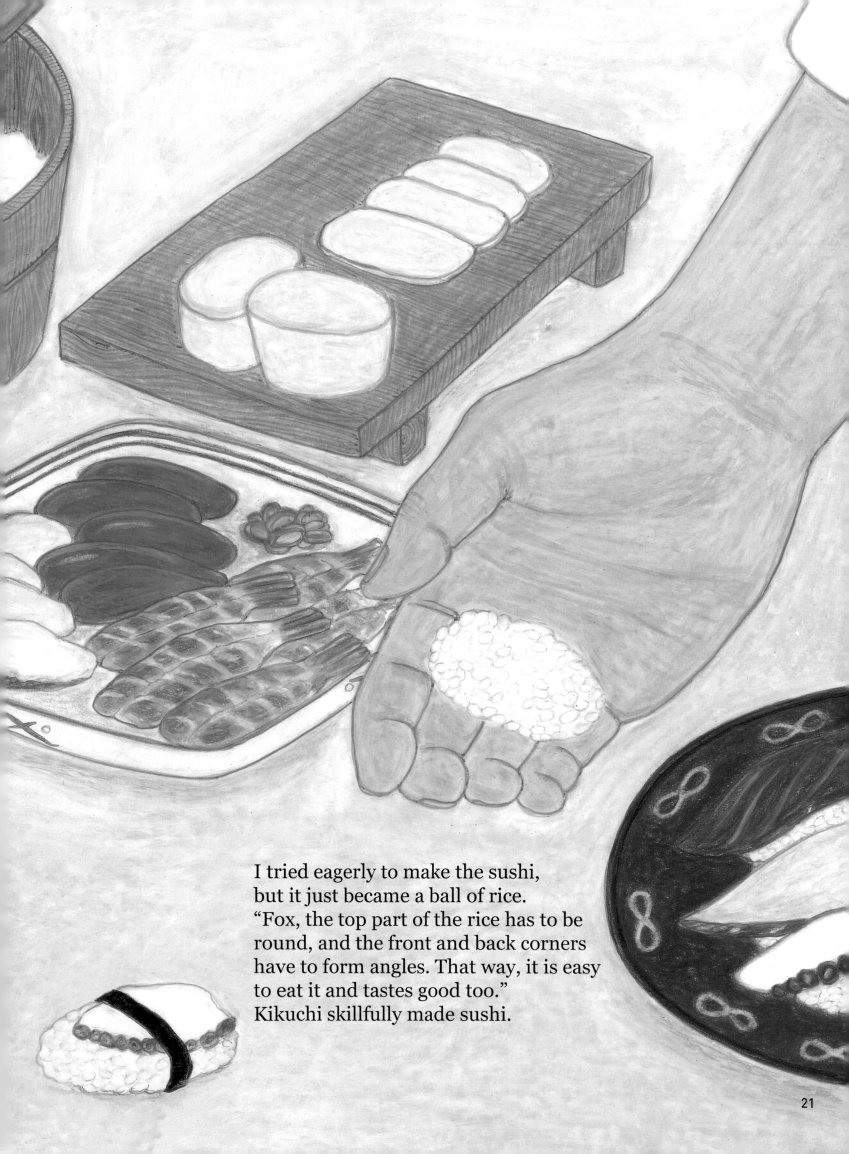

I tried eagerly to make the sushi,
but it just became a ball of rice.
"Fox, the top part of the rice has to be
round, and the front and back corners
have to form angles. That way, it is easy
to eat it and tastes good too."
Kikuchi skillfully made sushi.

"Fox, your hands are small, so why don't you try making a
rice ball instead of sushi? You can put a Japanese apricot,
pickled fish, and other ingredients inside of it."
I gathered more rice, made it round, and slipped in an
apricot and pickled fish eggs. I then tightly gathered the
rice to make a triangular rice ball.
"Here is a packed lunch," Kikuchi said. "Eat it tomorrow."
Kikuchi wrapped the lunch in a bamboo leaf, along with
warm miso soup.
I leaped for joy on my way back to the forest.

The next day, it rained for many hours.
The rain made every part of the forest wet.
"Brrr, it's cold."
I shivered as I waited in my cave for the rain to stop.
"I'm so glad I have the packed lunch," I said
to myself.
I unpacked the lunch Kikuchi had made me and
began to eat.
I enjoyed the sweet-and-sour taste of the pickled
fish eggs inside the rice balls.
The saltiness of the miso soup was delicious.
My stomach was happy and my entire body
warmed up.

Japan's Bento

Japanese cuisine focuses on appearance as much as the taste, so the lunch boxes, or bentos, are prepared very attractively. The bento called ekiben, which is sold in train and bus stations, is especially famous for being stylish and prepared using local produce.

After the rainfall, the forest was full of food to eat,
so I didn't visit Kikuchi's house for awhile.
One day, a thought came to my mind.
"Ah, I wish I could eat Kikuchi's sushi. I better go
and see Kikuchi tomorrow."
But for some reason Kikuchi was standing in the
middle of the forest. Huh? "Kikuchi! What brings
you to the forest?" I asked.
"Fox, today is a matsuri, a festival held in the
village. I came to go with you."
Kikuchi smiled and presented me with a package.

Japan's Festivals: Matsuri

In Japan, festivals are called matsuri. Every region has
a special matsuri, and during the festival, people pray for
things like their family's health, for the harvest to go well,
to catch a lot of fish, or for their business to prosper.

27

"Wow, it is so beautiful!"
Inside the package, there was a pretty kimono and a pair of Japanese wooden clogs.
I wore the kimono and a white veil around my face and went down to the village. No one was able to recognize me.
The matsuri was fantastic.
I went to a shrine to say a prayer and ring a bell.
I saw people marching while shouting and carrying a palanquin.
Kikuchi gave me cute candies that looked like rabbits.
"They are too precious to eat!"
They were sweet enough to make my mouth tingle, but were still very delicious.

After it got dark, the fireworks finally began.
Bang! Boom! Crackle!
My heart was pounding.
I will never forget the special memories
that I made with Kikuchi. I closed my eyes
and made a wish: to be able to eat Kikuchi's
sushi for a very, very long time.

Stories about
Japan shared by the Fox

Capital: Tokyo

Language: Japanese

Natural Environment: Japan's mainland consists of four main islands and has more than six thousand small islands. There are a lot of high, rugged mountains and Japan often has earthquakes and volcanic activity. It has four distinct seasons.

The red circle on the flag indicates a rising sun.

Tokyo

Where is Japan located?

Japan is located in eastern Asia. Hokkaido Island, which is the northern island of Japan, is south of Russia's Sakhalin Island, and Japan's southern islands stretch almost to Taiwan. Southern Japan faces South Korea, across the Sea of Japan and the Korea Strait.

What kinds of people live in Japan?

Various ethnic groups live in Japan. They can be separated into two groups. The northern ethnic group includes people from Mongolia, Korea, and parts of China, and the southern ethnic group includes people whose ancestors were from Southeast Asia or the South Pacific region. The southern ethnic group is much larger by population.

Tell me about some famous places in Japan!

Tokyo, which is the capital of Japan, is very prosperous and active.
Mount Fuji is located about two hours away from Tokyo, and it is the largest mountain in Japan. When the weather is nice, it can even be seen from Tokyo. The snow on top of the mountain never melts.

This is Mount Fuji.

Kyoto was the capital of Japan for more than a thousand years before Tokyo became the capital. Its natural beauty and a variety of cultural attractions make the city a popular field trip destination for students as well as foreign tourists.

This is the Golden Pavilion, located in Kyoto.

Tell me something that Japan is proud of.

Japan produces a lot of books. Among those books, comic books are the most popular. Japanese comic books are called manga. Manga is famous throughout the world. Not only does Japan publish a lot of manga, but they also film a lot of animated movies and TV shows, called anime.
Dolls and stationery based on animated characters are popular as well. There are also a large number of Japanese manga artists who are well known throughout the world. As a result, Japan has many people who want to become manga artists.

Japan's most popular dish/cuisine, sushi

Sushi is a Japanese cuisine that is famous worldwide. Rice is rolled into balls and fresh fish or different ingredients are placed on top of the rice balls. Making sushi looks simple, but it requires a lot of special technique and care to bring out the true flavor.

How to enjoy delicious sushi

It is a good idea to start off your meal by eating the sushi made out of light-tasting fish. This is because if you eat this type of sushi after a greasy sushi, you can't properly enjoy its refreshing taste. So first eat the sushi that is made of fish with white meat, which is less fatty. After that, eat the red-meat fish followed by the blue-meat fish. The fish part of the sushi should be dipped into the soy sauce. If the rice is soaked in the soy sauce, the rice ball may fall apart or the rice grains may absorb the soy sauce, which can overwhelm the food with a salty flavor.

🍣 Various Types of Sushi

Tuna sushi

Different parts of the tuna fish have distinctive flavors. Most of the parts are soft and light-tasting.

Gizzard shad sushi

The gizzard shad meat for sushi is usually marinated in a mixture of vinegar and water. The sushi chef's talent is often judged on whether the right amount of vinegar and salt has been used.

Shrimp sushi

A tasty shrimp sushi can be made with vibrantly red, fresh shrimp. It is popular because of its unique taste and chewy texture.

Sea urchin/Uni sushi

Sea urchin sushi, or uni, smells like the sea. Sushi that is rolled with dried seaweed like this is called a battleship roll, or gunkanmaki, because it resembles a battleship.

Egg sushi

For egg sushi, the egg is cooked until it is moist and soft like fluffy bread. The ingredients are easy to find, so it is a very common sushi.